Little Muddy Bear

S. Haggarty

authorHOUSE®

AuthorHouse™
1663 Liberty Drive, Suite 200
Bloomington, IN 47403
www.authorhouse.com
Phone: 1-800-839-8640

First published by AuthorHouse 11/13/2009

ISBN: 978-1-4389-4071-7 (sc)

Library of Congress Control Number: 2009901365

Printed in the United States of America
Bloomington, Indiana

This book is printed on acid-free paper.

Dedication

This book is dedicated to Karen Taylor, who passed away peacefully in her sleep after her struggle with cancer. I will always remember her courage, her strength, and her gift of laughter.

I love you, Karen.

Introduction

"That is it! I have had enough. I am running away from home!"

"I just can't take it anymore. The dog is jealous of me. He bit my ear off and the cat isn't any better. She scratched my eyes out and I had to have them repaired. I am just a bear."

"Sometimes all I do is sit upon a shelf, collecting dust for months. It is bad for me. It makes me cough. Then the dog comes in and tosses me about, biting my ears and face, ripping my seams and I scream, won't you please stop! But the dog keeps on going and I start to cry. Then the cat comes by and claws at my eyes. No more abuse; I am leaving. I am going to live in the forest. I am going to run away!"

"While everyone is downstairs, mid-afternoon, I will make my move."

"My life has just begun."

Table of Contents

Chapter One

~ Bear Escapes into the Forest ~

He hops off the shelf, lands on the floor, and then moves a chair from a desk to the other side of the wall by the open window, next to a closed door. He climbs up the chair, looking around, to see how he can reach that ceiling fan twirling around and around. He climbs from the chair onto a bookcase. The open window is still too far away. He reaches the top of the bookcase and does the only thing he can do—he looks down. What a mistake! He loses his balance and almost falls on his face. He's never liked heights. He's so scared. He has to be brave now to make his escape. He closes his eyes and takes a running leap. Through the air he goes, wheeeee, what a rush, as he grabs on to the blade of the fan, hanging on for dear life. He begins to get dizzy, whooshing around. He spots the window and counts down from ten. When he reaches number one, he lets go, hoping he'll land somewhere soft. Thinking to himself, he says, please … pretty please, don't let my bear body break. He bounces against the pole lamp and hit the windowsill with a thud, almost flying right out the second-story window. His front paws hang on for dear life as his hind legs scramble to get his bear body on the windowsill.

He lets out a huge sigh. What a relief. He smiles to himself and mutters, "I am so proud of myself." He pats himself on the back, as he stands on the last hurdle between his old world and new adventure. He takes off his silly clothes, for he is a bear; he doesn't need them. He raises his arms up high in the sky and takes a big breath of fresh air.

"Yippee, freedom at last!" he yells out with a great joyful cry. He is so very happy.

He sees, not too far away, a ladder leaning against the house. Using his natural climbing ability, his paws guide him along the eaves trough, and down the ladder he goes.

Once on the ground, he finally relaxes a little bit. There are no humans around so he knows for the moment he is safe and sound. The air is so fresh and cool, the sun is shining, blue skies fill his eyes, and green grass tickles his toes. It is a beautiful day, he thinks to himself. He is so glad to be alive.

The house is an old farmhouse that backs right into the forest. There he spots some flowers in a flowerbed. "Oh, they are just so pretty," he whispers, as he leans over to smell each and every one. Then he sees some birds in a tree. They are in a nest and they are chattering away. He wonders what all the fuss is about! He climbs up the old oak tree and is greeted by a big, cranky bird. She looks at him and says, "What do you want?"

"Um … I just wanted to know why all the birds in the nest were making so much noise?"

"Because it is close to feeding time," she says. "Now please be on your way. You are causing a stir with my babies."

"Oh, okay." He hurries on back down the tree. He's seen enough here. He is going to wander in the forest and start his journey.

He walks through the grass. It feels very soft upon his paws, and the warmth of the breeze blows at his fur every which way. With so much to see, he starts his journey on the path. He walks and walks, getting deeper and deeper into the forest of green. Pretty soon he starts to get a little bit hungry. The forest is rich in berries and fruit … yummy yum yum. He stops by a bush of berries. Mmmmm, so juicy and sweet. He fills his face and tummy with lots and lots of the delicious red berries, a delicious and tasty treat. Now he is sleepy. He thinks he needs a nap. So he picks a tree at the edge of the forest where the grass is lush, soft, and green like a bed. He lays his head against the tree and falls fast asleep.

Chapter Two

~ Two Squirrels and a Worm ~

Bear is having a nice sleep when suddenly something hits him in the head. "Ouch!" he cries. Then he hears giggling. Rubbing the goose-egg bump on his head, he looks up to see two squirrels staring down at him.

"Wake up, sleepyhead," they say. "It's daylight, time to get up." Yawning and stretching, he stands up. His tummy is rumbling. He has to get something to eat. That's when he notices it. As his eyes travel down to his toes, he sees a hole in his toe. "Oh no!" He mutters to himself. "I have to get that fixed or my stuffing will all fall out." But what can he do? He has no shoes. He goes for a walk to think about this. As he heads through the trees into the forest, he notices that everything is very green and fresh here. He loves his new home, and he loves being free. He walks down the worn path. It is a nice day, sunny and warm. Suddenly he hears someone walking behind him, and he turns around fast. To his surprise, it is the squirrels again. "Hey, what are you doing? That is my stuffing you're collecting. Give it back!"

"Stuffing, what is that?" they say.

"It belongs to me," says the bear.

"Well, we need it for our nest in the tree. Soon it will be fall and then it will be winter and things will be scarce."

"Give it back!"

"No!" they reply and start to run.

Bear doesn't stand for that. He runs after them. "Come back here!" he yells as he runs through the forest, jumping over tree stumps and logs. As the squirrels jump over a huge puddle of muck, bear tries to follow, but wipes out in the mud.

There poor bear sits covered from head to toe in mud. "Now what am I going to do?" he whispers to himself, and just then, he spots the squirrels sitting way up high in a tree. They make faces at him and giggle with glee. He stands up and tries to shake the mud off of his coat. Then he tries to climb the tree, but he cannot, as the mud has made his paws too slippery. Every time bear thinks he has a solid grip on the tree, he slowly slides down the bark and lands on his rump, squishing his tail. After each attempt, the squirrels laugh louder and louder. The last straw comes when bear's sixth attempt to climb the tree turns his body 180 degrees. He goes from looking at the top of the tree to looking straight down at the ground. Three paws give way, while one gets stuck in the bark, spinning him around, then down on his head he goes, falling to the ground. "Ouch!" he cries.

After rubbing his head, he sits down on a log and pouts with a frown on his face. Looking up at the tree, bear sees the squirrels jumping from branch to branch, tree to tree, until he can't see or hear them anymore. He looks down at the hole in his toe. He soon realizes that falling in the muck was a good thing, because it plugged up the hole in his toe. Now no more stuffing will come out. Not as long as he is covered in mud. He gets up and wanders over to a blackberry bush, and on one of the leaves he spots a little worm.

"Hello," says the little worm.

"Oh, hello," says bear.

"What kind of animal are you?" asks the worm.

"I am a bear," he replies.

"Well, what's your name?"

"Well, I don't have a name. I guess its bear," he says.

"That's not your name. That is what kind of animal you are!" the worm says.

"Oh," he says. "Then I don't have a name."

"But everyone needs a name. You can't go through life without a name. How will everyone know what to call you?" says the worm.

"Well then, what is your name?" asks bear.

"My name is Annabelle. I was named after my grandma."

"That's a nice name," says bear. "Are you here to eat berries too?"

"Oh no," she says, "I just eat leaves."

"Okay, good, let's sit here and have lunch together."

"Okay, bear," she says.

7

Chapter Three

~ Who Wants to Be my Friend? ~

Bear eats blackberries all day long, until he cannot fit another berry into his tummy. Then he dozes off and falls fast asleep. He awakes to find himself nestled right under the blackberry bush. Crawling out from under it, he feels the warmth of the morning sun. He is very itchy from the muck that is caked onto his furry coat. He stands beside a tree, scratching his back against the bark. What is he going to do today? Just then, he hears voices. A group of young bear cubs have joined paws and formed a circle. He crouches down beside the bush and watches.

Oh, he thinks, they have clothes on. They must be tame bears. Most of them are girls in frilly dresses. Some are off to the side with skipping ropes. Maybe they want to play hide-and-seek, he thinks. I will go over there and see. He marches over and makes himself look happy and cheery. Clearing his throat, out comes "Ahem."

They all turn around and stare at him. Feeling kind of shy, he says, "Hi, I am bear. Want to play hide-and-seek with me?"

"You're who?" says a girl bear in a frilly yellow dress.

"Bear," he replies.

"Oh," they reply.

"How come you all are dressed in clothes?" he asks.

"Because it is Sunday, and mother says we must look pretty to go to Sunday school," she says.

"What's Sunday school?" bear asks.

But before she can answer, a much older girl steps in and speaks. "We are not allowed to talk to strangers. Mother said."

"But I am not a stranger. I am a bear too."

"You're not a bear, you're more like a skunk," she says, pinching her nose. "Bears are not stinky and dirty, and they don't smell. Go make friends over there. Go find some skunks."

Bear turns around and walks away. "She called me a skunk," he says to himself. "That hurts my feelings." He wipes the tears from his eyes with his paw. He soon learns that not all animals in the forest are friendly. He sits himself down upon a rock, holding his head in his paws. What am I going to do? He thinks to himself. "No one wants to be friends with me," he says in a soft, muffled voice as he starts to cry. In the distance, he hears a little jingling sound. He wonders what is that sound?

He gets up quickly, and without making a sound, he peeks through the trees, to see a little wee bunny with a ribbon and bell around her neck. His eyes light up with glee. Maybe she will want to be friends. He tiptoes toward her as she eats the tender green grass. She looks up, startled. Bear says "Hello," as he sits down across from her. She is very busy chewing away. "Hello," he says again, but gets no answer. She is still nibbling away. "Do you know how to talk?" bear finally asks.

She swallows the tender grass. "Yup, I do!" she says.

"Then why didn't you answer?" he asks.

"Because it is rude to answer when your mouth is full!" she says.

"Want to play hide-and-seek?" bear asks.

"No, it is too late. I have to get home. My momma will be worried."

"Where is home?" he asks.

"Follow me," she says.

He follows her to a big farmyard two miles down the path. As he slips under the gate, his eyes light up. Standing before him is a huge white house.

"Come on," she says.

"Um, I don't know," says bear. "There are a few dogs there."

Chapter Four

~ Bear Meets Hank ~

Bear's eyes get as big as saucers as he sees Hank's head popping up over the fence. "Don't be scared, he won't hurt you!" says Bunny.

"How do you know that?" bear asks.

"Because Hank is my friend. He barks, that is how he talks to the other dogs."

"Oh," says bear.

"Besides, maybe he is barking because you look so funny."

Bear thinks for a moment, and then asks, "I look funny?"

"Yup, you do. You have all that goop on your fur."

"Oh, that," he says, looking down at his toe. "It's muck, not goop. I had to fix a hole in my toe, and I fell in the mud by accident, and it plugged up the hole in my toe."

"Why didn't your momma just sew it up?" Bunny asks.

"I don't have a momma," says bear.

"Oh, I am sorry bear." Bunny says.

"Sorry for what?" he asks.

"Sorry for asking."

"Oh, it is okay," he replies.

"Maybe you can stay for supper. Come on, I will ask Momma," Bunny says.

"But, what about the dogs?" bear cautiously asks.

"They won't hurt you. I will go first and you can follow. Oh, and just hop like I do. They will think that you are a bunny."

"Okay," he says.

Bunny hops quickly to the barn, with bear close behind. "Bunny, where were you?" Momma scolds.

"I was in the forest and met a friend who is lost."

Momma looks at bear. "What is that dreadful smell?" Momma asks.

"Oh, I guess it is me," bear says, looking down at his paws.

"What in the world is in your fur?" Momma asks.

"It is mud," Bunny says.

"Mud!" Momma says. "Why, you're not a pig! What are you doing in the mud?"

Bear explains his story as Momma listens.

"Can he stay for supper, Momma, please?" Bunny asks.

"Well, all right. Then he must go home," Momma says.

"But Momma, he has no home!" Bunny says. "Can we keep him? Please, please, please?"

"Maybe Alice will take him." Momma says.

"Who is Alice?" bear asks.

"She is the lady that owns this land. She lives in that big white house and she's such a dear lady. She took me in when I arrived, after she caught me eating her lettuce in the garden. She loves animals. That is how we all ended up here," Momma says.

Just then, old Hank walks in. "What is all the chatter about?" he says.

Bear looks at Hank and then runs behind Momma. "Don't be afraid. Hank is our friend and protects us all here."

Bear peeks out from behind Momma. "Howdy," Hank says.

"Don't be rude!" Momma says. "Say hello."

"Oh, hello Hank."

Momma tells Hank about bear's adventure and how maybe Alice will take him. Hank scratches his head with his hind paw before he lies down.

"Maybe we could make a plan, and come morning, we can put it in action," Hank says.

"Bear and Bunny, you go wash up. Dinner is on the table. Hurry now before it becomes too cold."

"Yes Momma," Bunny replies.

"Then get yourselves ready for bed. Soon it will be dark."

"Yes, Momma," Bunny says. "Come morning, Hank and I will have a plan."

Chapter Five

~ Bear Causes a Disturbance ~

Momma and Hank stay awake all night talking. Finally they decide that Hank would just carry bear in his mouth and scratch on Alice's door.

"It is the simplest way, I think," Hank says between yawns. Momma just nods her head. She was awake all night long, something she was not used to, and therefore very tired. Had she known the plan was so easy, she would have gone to bed long ago. She was just about to fall asleep when Wally the rooster started crowing.

"Cock-a-doodle-doo … Cock-a-doodle-doo," the old rooster crows. Bear, never hearing a rooster before, is alarmed. He jumps up from the spare bale of hay where he is sleeping, and starts running around frightening all the chickens in the henhouse. Feathers fly everywhere. He climbs down the ladder and searches for Momma. He runs all through the barn causing such a disturbance. Finally he hides behind Molly the cow. Startled, she kicks the pail over, making a loud crash. This startles the whole gang of dogs, who start barking, while bear hides in the corner. Led by Hank, the dogs are eager to find out what all the racket is about. Bunny, now awake, comes down the ladder and passes Hank and his gang on her way. "Oh no," she says. " bear is missing!"

She starts chattering to Hank at a hundred miles a second. Hank, of course, can't understand a word she is saying. Hank perks his ears up. "Bear is missing," she says.

"Missing?" Hank repeats. "What do you mean, missing?"

"I woke up and he was gone," Bunny says, as she wipes the fresh teardrops from her eyes. Bunny continues, "He is either hiding or I fear the worst, that maybe a wolf got into the henhouse and took bear."

"First, there is no wolf, Bunny," Hank says. "I was up all night with your momma. I would know if there was a wolf in here. I may be old, but I can pick up the scent of anything that does not belong here. I have a good honker," Hank says, pointing to his nose. Just then, Hank's ears perk up again. He listens and then says, "Here comes Alice! Quick, everyone act your normal self."

The hens start to chatter. The three families of bunnies line up in single file, trying to look their best. They all want to please Alice. As Alice reaches the barn, Hank gets up to greet her, wagging his tail. Her hand reaches out to pat his head. "That's a good boy," she says to Hank. She enters the henhouse, with Hank close behind her.

"My, my, my, look at all these feathers everywhere. I shall collect them all, and make some nice feathered pillows for the winter." She takes a small bag from her apron pocket and picks up all the feathers, putting them all in her plastic bag, returning them to her apron pocket. "I will be back later to collect the eggs," she says with a smile.

Bear, still in the corner, looks around. As she enters, she says, "Oh my, what is that terrible smell? It is like nothing I have ever smelled before."

Bear stands with his face pressing against the barn wall, as Alice calmly walks over to Molly. "Good morning, Molly old girl," she says cheerfully. She decides to investigate just where the smell is coming from. Her eyesight being poor, she doesn't see bear hiding in the corner. However, her nose tells her to look in the surrounding area of where Molly is standing.

Hank, not knowing that bear is there, helps Alice by sniffing out the area. When he picks up bear's scent, he walks away. Alice looks into Hank's eyes. "What did you find, old boy?" she asks.

Hank, wanting to protect bear, bows his head. Feelings of guilt swell into his throat. He has to tell Alice, for she saved his life, taking him in after his owner dropped him off in the forest to fend for himself. Hank finally found his way to Alice's farm after not eating for ten days.

It was Alice who took the old dog in, fed him, and nursed him back to health, giving him a place to live and the job to watch over the barn in case of predators. Hank lets out a small whine as Alice looks down at his pleading eyes. "What is it, old boy?" she asks Hank.

Hank slowly gets up, makes his way back into the corner, and gently carries bear to Alice's feet. Bear is afraid, and starts to tremble like a leaf, as Alice's eyes travel down to the floor. "What have you got, old Hank?" she says. The silence in the barn is almost overwhelming for Hank, as all the other animals form a circle around Alice, staring at bear lying on the wooden floor of the barn. "What is that?" she says.

Hank then picks bear up again and carries him into the sunlight outside of the barn. Alice follows close behind, as do the other animals in single file. Hank again drops bear, but on soft grass this time. "Oh my! What is this?" Alice says.

Turning bear over with her foot, she says, "Oh, it is a bear!" How did he get into the barn she wonders to herself. Being an animal lover Alice takes out her garden gloves from her pocket and picks bear up.

"Oh, you are a rather stinky little bear, but I think with a good scrubbing in the washing machine, you will come out just fine. Come now Hank, carry this bear for me onto the porch and I will wash him up." Hank obeys as he gently lifts bear up. Bunny's eyes fill with tears as she stands there watching bear disappear behind the porch door.

Chapter Six

~ Inside Alice's House ~

Hank puts bear down on the porch floor. Hank realizes that bear is anxious so he looks into bear's eyes and speaks in a calm voice. "Alice is a kind old woman. She will look after you. Don't be afraid, okay little bear?"

Alice comes in moments later and pats Hank on the head. "That's a good boy!" she says. "Now let's get bear into the bathroom. He is in desperate need of a good wash, and I know he is scared, so we will give him a bath instead of using the washing machine." Bear's eyes grow wide as he watches Alice filling the big tub with warm water. "Easy now, Hank. Just pick him up and sit him down into the warm water."

Sitting up in the tub with the warm water all around him, he feels warm and cozy. This isn't too bad yet, he thinks to himself. Alice takes out a white bath brush and leaves the room to fetch some things needed for the bath.

"Holy smokes!" he cries. "That's an awfully big toothbrush!"

"That's not a toothbrush," Hank says to bear. Hank can't help chuckling to himself. "It's to get that muck off your fur. Now hush, here comes Alice."

Alice returns with a fluffy bath towel and soap and bends down on her knees. Looking at the dirty bear, she says, "You need a good bath."

She begins to lather up his body with soap and bear likes the refreshing smell of the soap. He closes his eyes and relaxes.

Alice soaps up the bath brush and mixes it into a soapy lather. She gently glides it over his tattered fur, and the mud and dirt dissolve into the warm, soapy water. Alice unplugs the drain and says, "Now, little bear keep your eyes shut. I need to rinse the soap from your fur." She gathers two full buckets of warm, clean water and pours it slowly over bear's head. "There you go now," Alice says. "You are all clean."

She lifts little bear from the tub, wrapping him snugly in a fluffy, warm towel. Alice rubs his fur with the towel as she carries him into another room.

"Oh dear!" Alice says. "You've got a hole in your toe!" Bear had forgotten about his paw. "I will have to sew it up right away." Leaving him with Hank, she goes to find her sewing basket. Bear lies on the towel all stretched out and yawns.

"See, that wasn't so bad, was it?" Hank says.

Bear's little brown eyes look into Hank's eyes. "Nope, I enjoyed that. I have never had a bath before. It feels so good to be clean."

Meanwhile, back in the barn, Bunny sits on the bale of hay where bear had slept, and she pouts. "I sure miss bear, Momma," she says. "I wonder what Alice is doing with him."

Momma rubs her paws together and says, "bear is in good hands."

"But Momma, I never even had a chance to say good-bye," Bunny says, choking back sobs. Momma wipes Bunny's tears as they fall, and tells Bunny that it is okay to miss bear. Then she continues on, "Saying good-bye is never forever. Bear is just in Alice's care. He will be back, and I bet you won't recognize him. Just pretend that bear has gone on a vacation. Just like all the other bears in Alice's home. They go in all tattered and torn, and come back looking like new. Besides, Hank is with him. He won't let anything bad happen to little bear."

Bunny smiles and says, "You're right, Momma. Thank you for making me feel better."

"It's all a part of growing up Bunny," Momma says.

Alice returns with a basket filled with all sorts of goodies for sewing. She has all different colors of thread and buttons, bows, zippers, scraps of pretty material, pins, and needles. "Now this won't hurt a bit, little one," she says with a smile. "Easy now, it will just take a few minutes."

Bear really doesn't mind. He is very relaxed and lies very still for Alice while she stitches away. In a few minutes, Alice is finished. She runs a comb through bear's fur, and she uses her fingers to fluff it up. "Aren't you a sweetie," she says, smiling down at bear. She lifts him up into her arms and hugs him gently. Bear has never been hugged before, and he enjoys the love and affection Alice is showing him. She carries him off to another large room.

Hank follows close behind. Bear looks over Alice's shoulder with a big smile on his face. "You sit here for a while," Alice says, placing him on a cozy chair among the pillows. When she leaves the room, bear gets down from the chair. Wow! What a room, he thinks to himself. Standing on his hind legs in front of old Hank, he says, "I feel brand new!"

The room has gleaming oak floors, polished to a shine. Looking down, he sees his reflection in the floor. "Oh, hello other bear," he says to the reflection. "Look, Hank, another bear!" he says, all excited.

"That's not another bear, silly, that is you."

"Me?" bear says in disbelief.

"Yes, you!" Hank says.

"Oh, I look like that?" he asks Hank.

"Yes," Hank replies, "and it is much better than you looked when you first got here."

"Oh …" bear replies.

"You were chubbier then but now you're a lot smaller, more like a bear should look."

Bear, being very curious, looks around the room. The furnishings are richly carved and polished like the floor. He sees a loveseat, a few chairs and the shutters of a wide-open window, all in a cranberry color. What a pretty room, bear thinks to himself. "Umm, Hank … what is this room called?"

Hank thinks for a few moments, and then says, "This is Alice's sitting room. She comes here to read. I have to warn you bear, she will make some clothes for you that you will have to wear."

"But why?" asks bear. "I don't like clothes. Bears don't wear clothes," he protests.

"Domesticated ones do."

"What does domesticated mean?" bear asks.

"It means you are tame and friendly, and not a wild bear that eats humans. Wild bears are mean."

"Really!" bear says.

"Yes, of course," Hank replies.

"You mean because I have no clothes on, people would think that I am mean?"

Hank nods his head. "That is correct." "And you don't want people to think you're mean, because then they will be mean to you too."

"Oh, okay, I get it now."

Bear bends down and moves closer to Hank.

"Umm … what are you doing, little bear?" Hank asks.

Bear reaches behind Hank's head and embraces his neck, giving him a big hug. Then he says, "Thank you, Hank, for helping me. You're my best dog friend." Looking into Hank's eyes, he says, "There was a dog at my old home that was really mean to me. I am glad you're not a mean dog, even if you don't wear clothes."

Chapter Seven

~ A New Home for Bear ~

Later that evening, Alice makes certain she has bear's exact measurements. As bear and Hank whisper to each other in the dark, Alice is downstairs running her sewing machine. She is making bear some clothes, since he has none. The house is warm and cozy.

Gone are the days of sleeping on bales of hay. Bear misses Bunny terribly. He misses her cute nose that wiggled, and the evening chats with Momma.

"I wonder if Alice will ever let me play with Bunny again?" bear asks Hank.

"Of course Alice will let you play with Bunny, as long as you are a good bear. Just like tonight. I am sleeping in the house because I was extra good today. Did you know that out of the eleven dogs that guard the barn at night, I am the only one that gets house privileges?" Hank says with a grin. "Alice rewards us all for good behavior. The animals are free to go anytime they please, but they never leave. They know they have a good home here."

Hank stretches his legs and stands up.

"Where you going, Hank?" bear inquires.

"Nowhere. I am trying to get comfy. It is time we went to sleep bear."

Yawning, bear says, "I am sleepy too."

"Night, night, little bear."

"Good night Hank, see you in the morning."

And they both drift off to sleep.

The sun has just come up and Wally starts to crow. "Cock-a-doodle-doo."

Hank opens one eye and realizes that he is still in the house. He wanders out of the room looking for Alice.

He finds her sipping tea in the kitchen and he sits down at her feet, offering his paw.

"Good morning, Hank!" Alice says, reaching down to pat his head. "Where is our friend this morning?" she asks. "I made a nice yellow T-shirt for him to wear. We will brush his fur up all nice after we cut some off, and make him look cute as a button. Maybe he would like to visit the barn today. I bet they won't even recognize him."

"We will give him a new name too. Every bear should have a name. Why don't you go fetch him for me, Hank?" she says with a smile.

Meanwhile, upstairs, bear is already awake. Sniffing the air he scratches his head. A wonderful smell fills the room and his tummy growls. He is hungry. "Mmm, something smells good," bear says to himself. His mouth waters as he detects the smell of muffins. Holding his tummy, he sits up on the edge of the chair. Just then, Hank comes in, his nails clicking on the hardwood floor.

"Good morning, bear," Hank says.

"Good morning, Hank. What is that smell? Smells like berries, and I love berries."

"Alice is downstairs waiting. She asked me to fetch you. Come along, little bear."

"But how Hank? I don't really know how to climb down stairs."

Hank lies down in front of bear and says, "Have you ever ridden a pony?"

Bear looks surprised and says, "No."

"Well, climb on my back and hang on. That's it," he says to bear. "Now grab a hold of my neck, because here we go."

"Giddy up!" says bear, as they go galloping down the stairs.

Like a bolt of lightning, Hank runs so fast that he doesn't see the cat sitting at the bottom of the stairs. Leaping right over her, he is unable to stop as he slides across the kitchen floor, finally skidding to a halt right in front of Alice's feet. Bear, on the other hand, is jolted forward, and falls right into Alice's lap.

Alice smiles and says, "Hello, bear, how are you feeling this morning?" Bear spots a plump muffin in Alice's hand. He nudges her hand and she breaks off a few pieces, feeding it to bear. Hank, feeling left out, decides he will whine a little for he is hungry too. Alice sets a bowl down in front of old Hank, filling it with meat and gravy. Hank gobbles it up quickly, licking the bowl.

On the table in front of Alice is a new yellow T-shirt, a small blue brush, a comb, and scissors to cut bear's fur for his first haircut. Bear eyes the scissors. "Today you will look like a new bear. We will make improvements from yesterday," says Alice. "You don't have much fur to cut, but I will give you a new hairstyle. Oh, silly me." Alice begins to laugh. "I mean a new fur style, since it is fur you have, not hair."

She starts combing bear's fur forward, snipping off the ends until it is piled high on his forehead. This makes bear look like he has lots of hair, and she gives him little bangs.

"My, what a handsome little bear you are. Now it is time for you to put on this nice yellow T-shirt I made." Alice takes it, putting it over his head as she glides his paws in through the arm holes. It fits perfectly, and bear likes the color. It is nice and sunny-looking. Hank grins, thinking bear looks so cute, even better than yesterday.

"Now we can go out to the barn and visit," she says. Bear can hardly wait to see Bunny and Momma and the rest of the gang. Bunny is outside of the barn in the warm sun, munching on the last of the greens. Seeing Alice's door open, she hops into the barn as fast as she can, yelling, "Momma, Momma, here comes Hank and Alice and some other friend!"

Momma and the rest of the animals all head out into the barnyard. Bunny can hardly wait to ask how bear is!

Not recognizing bear, she hops right by him, and up to Hank. "Where is bear? Where is bear?" she asks Hank.

"He is with Alice, of course, Bunny."

"Where?" says Bunny. "I don't see him."

Looking very confused, Hank says, "That is him in the yellow."

Bunny's big eyes look past Alice to see bear smiling at her.

"That's him, Bunny." Hank points with his paw.

Just then, Alice turns around and says, "Oh, how nice, all the animals are outside for a change. This will make it easier to collect my eggs. Bear, you stay here with Hank while I collect the eggs." Bunny slowly makes her way to bear, and she sniffs his leg.

Bear laughs and laughs. "Stop it that tickles."

"Bear," she says, "is that really you?"

"Yup, it is me," says bear.

Bunny is overjoyed as she jumps up and down knocking bear over. "Yippee, yippee," she yells, and pounces on top of him. "I am so glad you are back. I missed you so much!"

Just then Momma comes over, her paw covering her mouth. "Oh my gosh, what a handsome bear," she says, "and no more stinky smell."

Sniff, sniff … "Hmmmmm, nice and clean, just like the laundry Alice hangs out on the clothesline."

"Come on," says Bunny, "let's go play hide-and-seek in the meadow. You too, Hank!"

The day was spent in the meadow, just the three of them, bear, Hank and Bunny.

Later in the afternoon, as Alice is taking the clothes off the clothesline, she thinks to herself, a name, a name, that little bear needs a name. The three had returned from the meadow to find Alice in the kitchen with muffins. They all sit at the table, except Hank. Bunny nibbling on a carrot muffin, bear eating his berry muffin and Hank crunching away on his Milk Bone treats.

All of a sudden Alice shouts, "I've got it, I have finally got it." "Got what," says Hank. "I have a name for bear. I think that we will call him *Little Muddy Bear*. Yes, I like that. From now on his name will be Little Muddy Bear. What do you all think of that?" Hank and Bunny smile and loudly cheer, "hooray, bear now has a real name!" A warm feeling flows through bear; at last he has a name.

Later that evening, as they all sit on the porch watching the sun set, Little Muddy Bear thinks about how far he has come and how excited he is about his new home. He feels very lucky to be a part of a family that loves and cares for him, as much as he loves and cares for them.

There were sure to be many happy days ahead for him at Alice's farm. This was just the beginning of a wonderful life for the *Little Muddy Bear.*

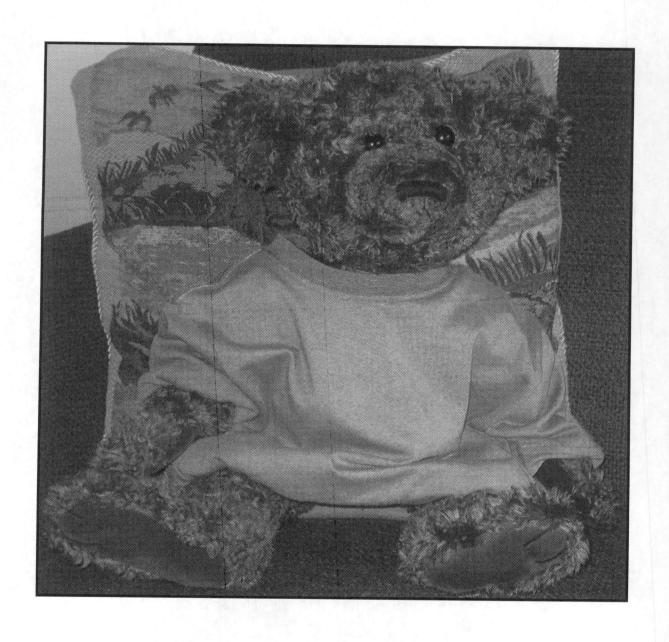